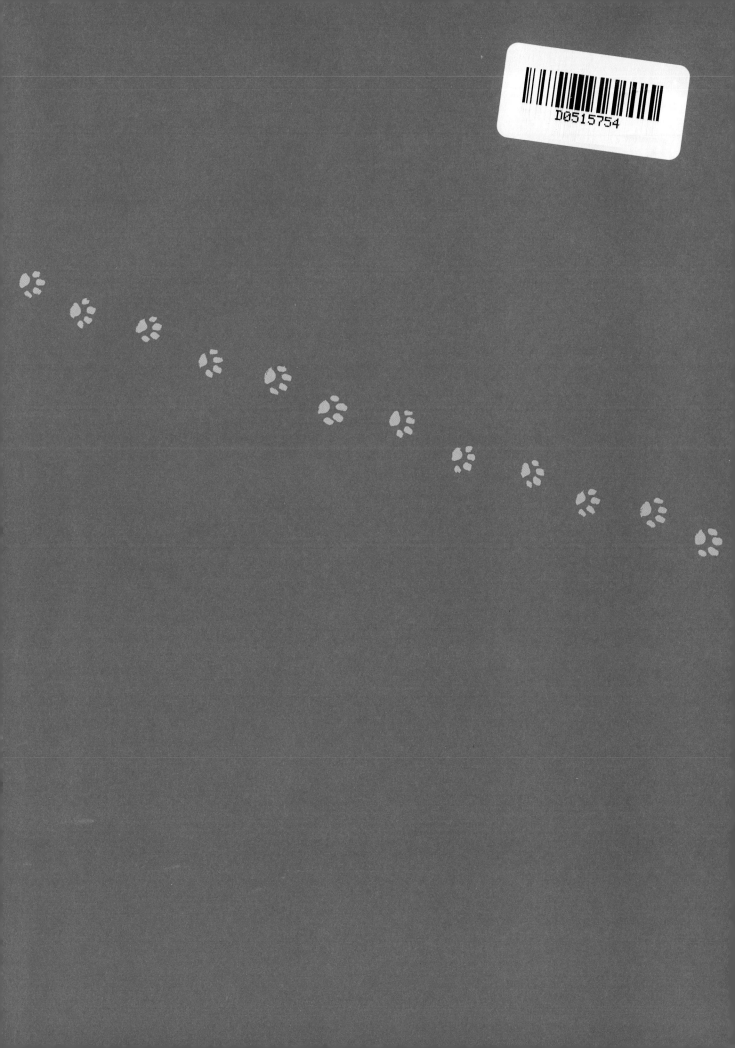

SUN

JUN

ALISON OLIVER

CLARION BOOKS | Houghton Mifflin Harcourt | Boston   New York

CLARION BOOKS
3 Park Avenue
New York, New York 10016

Clarion Books is an imprint of Houghton Mifflin Harcourt Publishing Company.

hmhco.com

The illustrations for this book were executed in watercolor, brush pen,
charcoal, and collage and assembled digitally.
The text was set in M Twentieth Century.

Library of Congress Cataloging-in-Publication Data
Names: Oliver, Alison, author, illustrator.
Title: Sun / Alison Oliver.
Description: Boston ; New York : Clarion Books, Houghton Mifflin Harcourt,
[2019] | Summary: Sun loves playing soccer but after seeing his brother,
Pablo, making art he goes on an adventure with a fox and reconnects with
his creative side.
Identifiers: LCCN 2018035181 | ISBN 9781328781628 (hardback)
Subjects: | CYAC: Creative ability--Fiction. | Imagination--Fiction. |
Foxes--Fiction. | BISAC: JUVENILE FICTION / Animals / Foxes. | JUVENILE
FICTION / Art & Architecture. | JUVENILE FICTION / Boys & Men. | JUVENILE
FICTION / Social Issues / Emotions & Feelings. | JUVENILE FICTION / Sports
& Recreation / Soccer. | JUVENILE FICTION / Nature & the Natural World / Environment.
Classification: LCC PZ7.1.O459 Sun 2019 | DDC [E]--dc23
LC record available at https://lccn.loc.gov/2018035181

Manufactured in China
SCP 10 9 8 7 6 5 4 3 2 1
4500750278

Sun was a star.

A soccer star.

He loved the game,
he loved the cheers.

But something was missing.

His brother was busy making art.
He looked happy.

Sun decided to take his ball
down to the beach.

He thought about his brother.
Sun used to make art too.

As he walked, he noticed
all the things the ocean
had washed out.

He climbed up and down the dunes.

Then he saw something unusual.

A little house!

It was mysterious.

It was magical.

How did it get there?

All of a sudden . . .

. . . he was nose to nose

with a fox!

Fox ran down the dune
to the water's edge.
Sun followed.

Fox showed him how to trot.

How to dive.

How to find things.

How to create.

Together, they made
a robot.

A sundial.

A dragon.

And finally, an entire galaxy.

Soon the sun began to set.

Sun and Fox sat together
and watched.

Sun listened to the waves
and felt the breeze on his face.
He felt connected to everything.

Then he noticed the
shadow on the sundial.
It was late!

Time to go.

Back home, Sun and Pablo
got to work.

And it was magical.